Seeking An Amish Man

Sarah Amberson

Published by Trellis Publishing, 2021.

SEEKING AN AMISH MAN

First edition. July 11, 2021.

ISBN: 979-8224006564

Written by Sarah Amberson.

SEEKING AN AMISH MAN

SARAH AMBERSON

The throbbing of the music was making Megan's head hurt. She glanced at her watch. It was nearly morning. She had been at the party for the whole night. She had had too much to drink and waves of nausea threatened to overwhelm her.

Her partying lifestyle wasn't something she was particularly proud of. It was something that she had started to do because all of her friends did it and she also had no reason not to.

Her mother had died the previous week. Now she had nothing left. She was all alone. Every single remnant of her family or people she loved were dead. She didn't know what to do with herself. In fact, she didn't know what to do with anything. The apartment that she had shared with her mother was still sitting there, just as she had left it that day when her mother had passed away. She hadn't done anything to clean it out. She no longer wanted to live there now that she was alone.

She hadn't realized just how sick her mother was, and when she had passed, it had been too late. She had somehow thought that her mother would beat the cancer that was eating her away.

"Are you all right?" Her best friend Christy was staring at her with concern in her eyes.

"I'm fine. You know what? I'm going to head back a little earlier than normal. I need to get some stuff done."

"You? Get stuff done?" Christy laughed harshly. Megan tried to remember why Christy was her friend again, but nothing was coming to mind. Maybe it was the alcohol in her system.

"I have a headache. I'll see you later." Megan hurried toward the exit and out on to the street before Christy could say anything else or stop her. Not that she really expected Christy to stop her.

The air in the street was fresh and cool on her flushed face. Megan leaned up against the wall of the building and put her hands on her knees, letting the vibrations of the music that was still playing race through her while she pulled in huge gulps of fresh air.

When she felt as if she wasn't dizzy anymore and would be able to walk in a straight line, she started walking. She wasn't sure where she was going. They were on the very edge of town and the street she took went further and further into the woods that surrounded the town.

Megan laughed out loud. On a normal day, she would be afraid to go into the woods alone, but the alcohol she had drunk was making her numb to it all. She couldn't think straight and at this moment, she didn't care about anything except getting away from the sound of the party and feeling better.

At some point she stumbled away from the road and into the woods. As the sun began to rise, she realized just how beautiful nature was. It reminded her of the walks she would take with her mother when she was a little girl.

Her mother had always enjoyed nature, at least when Megan was young. She had always been taking her on walks, to the zoo, to the lake and every other sort of nature type place that a person could imagine. She had so many memories of the things that they had done together, and it sent a stab of pain through her heart to recall them.

And then cancer had gotten to her mother. At first, Megan hadn't even been aware that her mother was sick, but she slowly found out when she saw her throwing up, when she started visiting the hospital all the time, and when she eventually started losing her hair.

Her mother had pretended she was going to recover. She had tried to shield her from the reality of how bad it really was. When Megan had found out that her mother was actually dying, everything had spiraled out of control. And then she had died and left Megan all alone.

She regretted a lot of the things she had done now, wishing that she could go back in time and take them back. She had begun to hang out with the wild crowd and go to parties. It had been a distraction from the pain that gripped her heart, but she hated it too. Megan sighed and let herself slide down a nearby tree.

It was a large oak tree with large branches full of leaves Little bits of sun filtered through the spaces in the leaves, making it feel almost like a wonderland as she looked straight up into the sky. Birds were flying from branch to branch calling in their high - pitched voices to one another. It was a different world out here in the woods and Megan wondered why she hadn't ever noticed it before.

Megan laughed and let her hands fall down by her sides. As she did so, her hand fell against the corner of something hard. Surprised, she pulled her hand back and leaned forward to investigate. It was a small rectangular lockbox. It was metal, heavy, and painted black. Megan brushed the leaves away that had been concealing it and pulled it unto her lap. She expected to see a padlock closing it, but it didn't have one. She shook it to see if there was something inside and heard the sound of papers shifting.

She looked at the box with a moment of trepidation. She wasn't sure what she would find inside. What if it was something bad or dangerous? Or what if there was a terrible secret someone had hidden in there? She looked all around her. It had to belong to someone. Why would a box like this be out alone in the woods?

She shook her head and reached toward the lid. Any fear she had was pushed back to the back of her mind. She couldn't afford to be afraid right now. After all, it wasn't like you found something like this in the forest every day.

She lifted the lid up slowly, until it revealed its contents. Inside, was something she certainly hadn't been expecting. There was a stack of letter envelopes. Some of them looked wrinkled and older, as if they had been there quite some time but the ones on top looked newer, as if someone had just picked them up from the store a few days ago.

Megan knew that this was private and probably belonged to someone, but at this moment, she wanted to know what the box was about. As she shuffled around in its contents, her hand pulled out a few photographs on the side of the box.

There was one of a young couple standing together. They looked younger than her, probably sixteen or seventeen. The young man was very handsome. He had dark brown curls that fell over his eyes. His cheeks were round, but also structured, and his blue eyes sparkled with amusement, even in the photograph.

Megan almost felt as if he were staring back at her. The young woman was beautiful too. Megan was surprised to realize that she actually looked sort of like Megan herself, but she was wearing a dress and gold earrings. She looked to be about 18 or 19 years old.

She had long brown hair that tumbled down her back, laying in gentle curls that made her want to run her fingers through them. She had blue eyes that were full of mischief and a smile with a dimple on her cheek.

She was looking up at the boy who was about a head taller than her. Megan might not know much about love, but she knew that this girl was in love. Her entire face was practically glowing with it.

She looked through the rest of the pictures. Most of all, it was pictures of the same two people. Sometimes they were together, and sometimes they were apart. It the pictures where they were together, they both looked as if they were the happiest two people in the world.

Curiosity taking her over completely, Megan dug into the box and pulled out the envelopes. They appeared to be letters of some sort. The only thing written on the envelopes was the date, nothing more.

Megan opened the oldest one. It was from nearly nine months ago. They weren't sealed, so she wasn't worried about whoever they belonged to finding out that she had snooped. She unfolded the two pieces of notebook paper carefully and began to read the neat handwriting.

My dearest Ellen,

It's been nearly three months since we buried you. I struggled with this since the moment I lost you. I wanted to let you go like I promised, move on and never look back, but I just couldn't.

Every single night when I close my eyes, your face is there, staring back at me. Where did I go wrong to deserve such cruelty, Ellen?

I need you. My world is dark and ugly without you. I look at your pictures every time I come here, imagining you could jump out of them and be here with me again.

I know that the Amish don't approve of pictures. I know that the deacon wouldn't approve of me having them if he found out. Goodness, I'd probably get shunned if I got caught. But the time that I spent with you, I can't throw it away. Even though I am nearly nineteen now, I feel as if I was just meeting you in Rumspringa yesterday.

I haven't joined the church yet. No one has pressured me because they know I am grieving. They don't know who you were or why you died. All I have told them is that my best friend died at the end of Rumspringa. I will have to make a decision soon. How can I stay here where I no longer feel as if I belong? But also, how can I go out there into that world when I don't have you to guide me?

You will always have all of my love,
Martin

Megan blinked her eyes, sending the tears that were there on the surface back to where they had come from. She had learned so much about Martin and Ellen just by reading this first letter. She found herself reaching for the next one, even though her aching heart was telling her to stop.

My dearest Ellen,

I wonder sometimes if you are staring down at me from heaven?

May reread the line three more times. It was just one single line. She wondered why he had written so little that day. Maybe it had been a bad day for him, and he just didn't have the time to sit down and write. She wondered if this young man still came here to write letters to Ellen.

She glanced around again, trying to spot anyone in the woods. She could see for quite some distance through the spaces between the trees, but saw no one. She wondered what this mysterious Martin would do if he caught her reading his private letters.

She pulled out the third letter, hoping that it would have more about the tragic story of Ellen and Martin.

My dearest Ellen,

Your mother came to my house today. My parents wanted to know why she was there in the Amish community, but she refused to talk to anyone but me. She wanted to know how you died. I thought that the police would have told her, but apparently, she wanted to know what I knew since I was close to you when it happened.

I told her about the accident, about how we never meant to get hurt when we took your uncle's car and went driving.

I told her about the song we were singing on the radio when we weren't paying attention to the road. I wonder sometimes if I had made sure that you weren't drunk when we left the party if things would have happened differently.

She knew about the semi, how we didn't see it and how it turned in front of our car. I thought she would hate me, but she didn't. She gave me a hug and we both cried. We miss you, Ellen.

If I could have traded places with you that day, I would have. I know that only two people died in the crash that day, but sometimes I feel like I died too and all three of us are dead.

I hope that Matt is up there, looking out for you.

I love you,

Martin

Megan leaned back for a moment, trying to imagine what it would be like. Suddenly, guilt overtook her. She had been drunk and driving more than once. She realized that what she was doing was dangerous, but she had never had a real reason to stop. What if she unwittingly killed someone while driving drunk? She could never forgive herself if that happened.

She wondered if Ellen would have known she would have died that day because she was drinking alcohol if she would have still drunk it. Megan had a feeling that she wouldn't have.

The pulled out he fifth letter. It was short, kind of like the second one.

It's been nearly six months, Ellen. I miss you so much. I have no one to talk to that could possibly understand. Most of the young people stay away from me. I feel like I am slipping away a little more each day. I want this all to end. I want to forget this happened.

Megan didn't know what to think of this letter. It was so short and yet so full. She wanted to know if Martin was all right.

She hurriedly pulled out the next letter and realized that it was the last one. When she looked at the other envelopes, she saw that they were still blank, waiting for words to be put on them.

My dearest Ellen,

I feel like I have to stop writing to you. You will never read these, though maybe you can see me writing them from heaven and read over my shoulder. I'd like to think so anyway. Please tell God up there that I need help with something.

My parents are pressuring me to join the church. I keep thinking about our plans. We wanted to make a Christian family together and raise children. We wanted to live our own lives. I want to do that, but I can't do it alone. Will you hate me if I just stay in the Amish Community?

They aren't bad people. I don't dislike them. In fact, I love most of them. But I am not okay here. I am not at home. They don't understand me. But I don't know how to leave. I guess I will always be alone.

Send me a sign if you are out there and hear me, Ellen.

I love you,

Martin

Megan leaned up against the back of the tree, her drunkenness was turning into a severe hang-over and her head was pounding in pain. She felt sick all over like she always did when she drank too much. Why did she do this to herself? She started to close the box, and then paused.

She reached in and pulled out one of the envelopes on top. She reached down and picked up the black pen that was nestled into the bottom of the box and she started to write.

—-*—-

Martin walked down the path into the woods. It had been a while since had visited his box of letters. He wanted to forget they existed and move on with his life, but it was like it was his last tie to Ellen, pulling him there, demanding his attention.

When he arrived, he immediately noticed something was different. The box was in a slightly different place and was sticking out of the leaves. He bent down and dug out his box, hastily and quickly clutching it to his chest. What if someone from the church and had read the letters he had written and seen the pictures? He could be shunned or kicked out. He didn't know what the punishment would be.

He ran further into the woods, looking over his shoulder and around each tree, fully expecting to be caught at any second. When he had covered some distance, he stopped breathlessly and looked all around. But he saw no one. He sat down against a tree and slowly opened the lid, almost holding his breath.

He immediately noticed the new letter on top of the ones he had written. The envelope was blank except for his name in the center of it. His hand nearly shook as he reached out for it. He took his time opening it and unfolding the paper inside. The words were written in a beautiful hand. He read the words, unsure what to think of them.

Hello, Martin,

I know you have no idea who I am. Goodness, sometimes, I don't even know who I am. I was having a really bad day and stumbled upon your box here in the woods. I didn't mean to pry, but I read your letters.

They are beautiful. Nearly a week ago, my mother died. I feel like I have lost my will to live, losing the last person that I love. I have searched for meaning in my life, but have found none.

I had been at a party and I had been drinking. I am so sorry for what happened to you. Frankly, it frightened me to read about your Ellen dying after drinking.

I feel like I am walking asleep through every day, just waiting for the world to be over. Your words were such a wonderful story that it made me cry and it made my heart ache for you and Ellen.

It makes me want to be a better person to see your words of love. We will probably never meet, but one day, if we were to, I hope you know that there is still love out there for you somewhere. It may not seem like it, but somewhere out there, someone needs you.

Take care,

- M

When he was done, he felt his heart pounding hard in his chest. For some reason, he didn't feel angry. He almost saw these words as a sign from Ellen. By total chance, his words had reached out and helped someone.

He pulled out another piece of paper and began to write, but this time, it wasn't to Ellen.

—-*—-

Megan had kept away from the box in the forest for several days now. But the words that she had read in that box haunted her. She wondered who Martin was, what he looked like now, and if he was all right.

She had stopped drinking since she had read that story. She hadn't touched a drop, even though her body and her mind were begging for it. Eventually, she found herself walking towards the box's hiding place. She knew it was there and as crazy as it seemed, she wanted to know if the man had written back or even seen her letter.

She had dreamed of what it would be like to meet him, to see him and talk to him in person. She wondered... it was a crazy thought, but she wondered if someone like him could ever have feelings for her the way he had for Ellen.

When she arrived, she pulled out the box and was surprised to see that the top envelope was different than the one she had left there.

On the envelope, a single letter was written, "M"

Megan hurried to open the letter and read the words with growing hope, and emotion.

Hello M,

I don't know who you are or how you found my letters, but I want you to know that it was the most encouraging thing I have read since Ellen's death. At first, I didn't know how to respond, but I do now.

I know that we have never met, and you have no reason to believe anything I say, but I want to meet you. I want to see who you are and talk with you personally. If you would be willing, meet me at the bakery in the Amish town. I work there.

If you choose not to come, I will understand. The choice is yours and don't feel pressured. I feel like somehow, we are meant to meet one another. Sometimes God works in mysterious ways.

- Martin

Megan felt tears of joy threatening to spill over her cheeks. Of course, she wanted to meet Martin. In fact, she almost felt as if they were old friends, who knew everything about each other.

She didn't know exactly what he was thinking about her as. Maybe he was interested in her, but maybe he just wanted to meet the woman who had interrupted his privacy.

Either way, Megan didn't care. She had nothing to lose. She was going to meet Martin, and maybe, just maybe she could help him in some way. Maybe they had more in common with each other than they thought.

Megan practically ran home. When she got there, she took her time picking out the most modest clothes she had. She looked through her closet and in the back was a dress that belonged to her mother. It was long and came down almost to her ankles.

Megan put it on and gave a little spin, admiring the way that the soft yellow fabric flowed around her, like a gentle cloud enveloping her.

She opted for some white tennis shoes and tied her hair back in a low ponytail. When she was satisfied with how she looked, she headed outside and hurried toward the Amish community. Everyone knew where the little Amish community was. It was just that no one from her circle of friends really went there.

As Megan went, she tried to imagine all the different ways that this meeting would go. She knew that she didn't know Martin well, but somehow, she trusted him. From seeing his most vulnerable thoughts written out on paper in the woods, it made her feel as if Martin was a good man whom she could look up to, who would do nothing to hurt her.

When she arrived at the entrance of the tiny Amish town and continued down the street toward the bakery, she tried to keep herself from feeling self-conscious. She could feel people glancing at her, giving her strange looks, wondering why she was here. People from outside the community often bought baked goods there so she tried to hang onto that thought, hoping it would explain her presence.

She herself started to doubt why she was there when she arrived at the bakery. She stepped into the small building, her nervousness and anxiety growing. Maybe coming here had been a mistake.

There were no more customers in the bakery besides her and for a moment, Megan thought that she was the only one there at all.

But then a young man appeared from behind the counter. For a moment, Megan didn't recognize him, but then she realized that he was the same man from the photographs in the box.

He looked older and the happy spark in his eyes was gone, but he was still the same person.

"M, is that you?" the man who Megan supposed to be Martin asked.

"It's Megan actually."

Martin came around the counter with a look of fascination and curiosity on his face. He removed his apron and took a set of keys from his pocket. He folded the apron and placed it on the counter.

"Megan, that's a nice name." Martin had a deep soothing voice. Megan had a feeling that she could listen to him talk all day. "Do you want to go on a walk?"

Megan nodded, unsure of what else to say. She knew that anyone else would be afraid to be alone with this Amish man with the look full of pain in his eyes. But she wasn't. She had a feeling that something wonderful was going to come of this meeting. She suddenly had no more worries.

—-*—-

Martin glanced over at the young woman who was walking beside him. It was uncanny how much she resembled Ellen. Her dark brown hair was pulled into a low pony tail, moving softly from side to side with her gait as she walked.

Her expression was full of sadness and pain, very similar to how he felt. He wasn't sure of what to think, seeing her here. He hadn't really expected her to come when he'd written that letter. He had wondered how he would recognize her if she showed up at the bakery, but he had known the instant he laid eyes on her that she was the mysterious M.

He thought of why he had written that letter. He was supposed to join the church in a week's time and the thought that maybe, just maybe, getting to know the mysterious person behind the letter in his box might give him some guidance on what to do.

He had never thought that Megan would be such a lovely young woman. His heart stirred in his chest and he felt a bit of excitement rush through him. He didn't understand how he could possibly feel that way and for a moment, he felt a little bit of guilt. He wondered what Ellen would think of Megan or how they had met.

"So, did you have a hard time finding the bakery?" Martin asked.

"No, it was quite simple. Martin, I wanted to ask you something." Megan looked nervous.

"What is it?"

"I wanted to know, why did you invite me here exactly? What is it that you hope to accomplish by this? It's not that I am complaining. I wanted to meet you from the moment I read the first letter, but I just want to know why you would want to meet the person who read your private letters."

Martin looked down at Megan for a moment, trying to come up with a good answer to her question.

"You know, I am not really sure. When I first read your letter in my box, I kind of felt embarrassed that another person had seen the words I wrote, but then I realized that your words made me feel better." Martin took a deep breath. "I am sure that nothing I am saying is making any sense, but I feel like we have a connection, a strange odd connection that no one could understand."

Megan nodded, and just like that they began to talk. Martin told her about the difficulty of losing Ellen and how no one understood what they had shared. Megan told him about her mother and how her life had spiraled out of control after she had died and how she had stumbled across the box in the woods when she had escaped the party.

By the time that it was time for Megan to go home, it was late in the afternoon and Martin had hardly felt the time go by. He had enjoyed his talk with Megan. He had enjoyed every single moment of it, and he didn't want it to end. When they were back in front of the bakery, Megan looked nervous and was scrunching her skirt between her hands.

"Will you come back again?" Martin asked.

"Do you want me to?" Megan looked up at him, her eyes full of doubt.

"Yes, I do. I would like that very much."

Megan nodded and turned. "Ok then. I will come back in two days. Good evening, Martin, it was nice meeting you."

Martin watched her go, a little ache starting in his heart when he felt her absence. He had a feeling that today, they had started a friendship that would last for a long time.

—-*—-

Four months later

Megan hurried through the woods. Her heart felt light and her giddy smile couldn't get any bigger even if she wanted it to.

She had been waiting for this day since the moment she had met Martin. Of course, she hadn't known it back then. Back then he had been a mysterious stranger with a sad past that she had somehow been drawn to.

In the last few months, they had visited each other nearly every other day. Megan had enjoyed their conversation more than she had ever known possible. She had looked forward to every single moment they had spent together.

She had said goodbye to Christy and all of her old friends for that matter of fact.

She had stopped partying and dealt with her mother's apartment. She looked down at the soft blue dress she was wearing. Even though she and Martin had decided to leave the Amish, she had started to dress more modestly, and she honestly couldn't feel better about it. It made her feel feminine and delicate like a flower.

After what seemed like forever, she reached the place where all of this had started. Martin was standing there, a small suitcase on the ground beside him.

When Megan walked up to him, he pulled her close into a hug. Megan wrapped her arms around him.

"How do you feel?" She asked.

"Good. You know, when I first decided not to join the church and go out into the world, I was a little scared. But now that I am here, and now I feel free, excited even."

Megan gave a tight smile. "You know, if you want to stay with the Amish, I could stay too."

"No, the Amish are for some people, and I think that the people who live there enjoy it there. But some are not meant to stay, and that includes me and you, Megan. Let's go to California, just like we talked about."

Megan nodded, "What will we do with the box?" Both of their gazes landed on the little metal box that had brought them both together.

"You know, I was thinking about that. I think we should write one last letter."

"For who?" Megan was confused, she didn't mind if Martin wanted to write a last letter to Ellen, but he had told her that it was behind him.

"For whoever finds it. I think we should leave it here. You know, you stumbled across it and it helped you, and then it brought us together. Maybe my story and then our story, can help someone else."

Megan nodded, "I like that idea."

They sat down under the trees and Martin pulled out a blank sheet of paper and the pen, handing it to Megan.

"What should I write?"

"Whatever you want to tell the next person who finds it." Martin had that mischievous grin in his eyes. "I also brought this." He held out a small photograph strip to her.

It was the strip of photos that they had done together in a photobooth at the fair. Megan smiled. "You want to leave that in the box too?"

"Yes." Martin was nodding, a thoughtful look on his face. "Megan, you are a part of this story as much as Ellen and I are. You deserve to have you picture in here too."

Megan felt a tingle of warmth and love pass through her for Martin. She poised the pen over the blank page and began to write.

Dearest Reader,

I don't know if this will be read one day, or if it will sit here on the forest floor forever. But if it does get found, we thought we would give you some advice. If you have read the other letters in this box, you will be able to see that tragedy happens all the time in life.

You are going along fine and then you feel as if you have been pushed off a cliff and can't stop yourself.

Don't let yourself keep falling. The sadness, anger, and hurt only lasts for a moment unless you hold onto them. You should open your heart to new experiences and new people, because you never know when someone will flip your life around and fill your heart with happiness again.

Alcohol only drains the happiness from you and fills you with regret and illness. Leave it behind and find a person to show love to. Sometimes pain opens your heart to a new love. And sometimes God works in mysterious ways to bring people together who might not have ever met one another.

Martin and I found each other and we are here, sitting together, about to go to California and start a new life together, if you were wondering. We hope that whoever sees this will be encouraged by our story, and find a path of their own, despite the pain.

With Love,

Martin and Megan.

Megan set the pen down and folded up the paper gently, tucking it inside the envelope. She wrote the date on the front, making it neat and easy to read. She then handed it to Martin who set it into the box and buried the box under the leaves.

He stood and reached his hand out to her, "Shall we?"

Megan tucked her hand in his larger one and he pulled her up. The sun was starting to set. It was casting rays of pink and orange that mixed and made beautiful colors in between.

Martin looked down at her, "Megan. I know that we are friends, even more than friends, but I need to tell you something."

Megan paused and looked up at him. "What is it?"

"When we met, I was in a bad place, I was so alone and felt like I had no one left. And then you walked into the bakery. You were so beautiful and different, and it was like you carried a hundred rays of sunshine with you."

Megan felt her chest swell with happiness.

"When you started to visit me, and we started to talk, it was like we had this instant connection that just grew stronger with time. Megan, I love you and I hope that you have those feelings for me too. I thought it wasn't possible to love again, but I was wrong. I do love you."

"I love you too," Megan whispered. She had so much that she wanted to tell him, what she had thought of him since the first time she had read his name signed at the bottom of one of Ellen's letters, but she knew that it could wait. She leaned it and wrapped her arms around his waist, letting her head rest on his chest.

She felt safe and she felt happy in his arms. She felt like as long as they were together, as if nothing bad could happen to her while she was with Martin.

"Are we going to be okay?" She whispered.

Martin kissed the top of her head.

"We are going to be okay."

—-*—-

Martin closed his eyes, enjoying the moment of having Megan close to him. He loved her. He didn't know how it had happened, it had happened very slowly.

So slowly that he had barely noticed, but Megan had become a huge part of his life, she had become the one thing that kept him going. When he thought of all the things that had happened to him, or being depressed, he thought of Megan, the girl with sad eyes who also had bad things in her past, but was willing to overlook them so they could move forward.

He smiled as the sun ducked down lower in the sky. Their wedding had been simple, but they were together now, and the road stretched out before them. They were going to California, and there he had a feeling that they would have an adventure together and be happy, forever.

REBECCA'S AMISH DREAMS

25

Rebecca's eyes were closed tightly. In her mind's eye she saw a picturesque old farm house with beautiful lines, decorated to perfection, with a quaint sign swinging in the breeze: "Peaceful Farm Bed and Breakfast." Children weaved in and out of the fall decorations lining the path to the front steps, as men and women relaxed back in pairs of hand-crafted rocking chairs. A blue sky with fluffy white clouds was the backdrop to the property leading out to the neighbor's corn and wheat fields. She smiled and sighed as a sense of tranquility and hopefulness overwhelmed her mind.

"Rebecca."

"No, please."

"Rebecca, darling, open your eyes."

"Do I have to?"

Her mother, Esther, gave a throaty chuckle. "Yes, Dear. Open them up."

Rebecca opened her eyes and immediately lost the feeling. She was gazing at a two-hundred-year-old wreck. Well, maybe "wreck" was too strong of a word, but it certainly wasn't the picture that she had just summoned in her mind. It was run-down, with boards and shingles hanging loose. The porch had holes and there were certainly no rocking chairs anywhere in sight. The yard was overgrown with vines and tangled grasses. And as if that were not all bad enough, the pewter gray sky was threatening a true Pennsylvania storm.

"How did Grannie live here?"

"Well, it has been over a year since she was in the nursing home. I'm sure that you uncle did a great deal of upkeep on the house while she was away."

"But how could he let it get this bad? Did you know that it was going to look like this?"

"No, but your father's brother was never a kind individual, and if he knew, as the executor of her estate, that Grannie was going to leave the house to us, he wouldn't have spent any resources to care for it."

"How are he and Papa related?"

"Your Papa was a kind soul. I don't know why your uncle is the way he is."

"This is just so overwhelming to look at, Mama." Rebecca felt tired and crushed. After so much anticipation, this was a difficult reality to be faced with.

"I bet that the inside is better than it looks from out here," her mother said, forcing a chipper tone that Rebecca had no trouble seeing through.

The two women stood in silence for a few more moments, the dust from the dry road settling on the two suitcases that sat between them on the broken- up path to the front steps.

"This place looked so different in the pictures." Rebecca looked at her mother's profile. Her mouth hung slightly open and her shoulders seemed a bit hunched, as if there was something heavy on her back, as well.

"Yes, well, we haven't been back here in a very long time, Darling. Time has not been kind to the property."

There was a rumble of thunder as a strong wind screamed across the land, whipping their dresses around their ankles. Rebecca allowed herself one more sigh and then nodded her head resolutely. "Let's get in there and get settled, Mama."

Her mom nodded and they both grabbed their suitcases and carefully picked their way over the walkway, up the stairs and around the holes on the porch.

Rebecca reached into her deep dress pocket and pulled out the key that Cynthia, the secretary at the law firm overseeing the transfer of ownership of the estate, had given her that morning. She brushed away the dust and dirt from the lock, inserted the key and the lock clicked open. She took a deep breath, squeezed the handle and the door swung open slowly. She could make out the shapes of furniture covered by sheets, but there was very little light coming through the windows as the storm rolled in darker and darker clouds. She reached to the wall next to her and lit the lamp.

The two women made their way in and Rebecca carefully removed the sheets off of a couch and a chair so that they could sit down. They did so, careful not to kick-up too much of the dust that had settled all around the room.

As another clap of thunder shook the house, a bright bolting of lightning lit up the windows, even through the grime-covered panes. A torrent of rain began in earnest outside the window and Rebecca leaned back in her chair. "Well, Mama, at least we have somewhere dry to wait out the storm."

And even as those words left her mouth, Rebecca heard the sound of dripping water in the corner of the room.

"Darling, go into the kitchen and find a bucket, we have a leak," her mother said calmly.

That first afternoon and evening in the house was a tiring time. They went from room to room, lighting lamps and taking stock of what each room would need. Their goal had been to be up and running for business within four months, prior to the bad winter weather, and they were going to try to stick to it. They would assess the needs for the outside of the home in greater detail the next day, they decided, as the rain continued to pour down. There was certainly a great deal of work to be done, but they were pleased to see that many of the bedrooms would require little more than tasks they were able to complete on their own – cleaning, painting, simple carpentry. For the larger jobs they would need to hire help, but they would plan to do as much work on their own as possible.

As the night crept in around them, the rain stopped and the stars actually came out. Rebecca found two side-by-side rooms that were in the best shape and set to cleaning them up so that she and her mother could settle in for the evening after dinner. Her mother fixed a simple meal on the stove in the kitchen, and they ate together in silence on the sturdy, covered portion of the porch, both thinking their own thoughts.

After dinner they cleaned up and headed to the bedrooms that Rebecca had prepared. "Darling, it is going to be wonderful. Remember this is our great adventure, right?" Her mother's tired eyes were hopeful as she looked at Rebecca.

"Of course, Mama, this will be the best adventure ever." She smiled the best smile she could manage and entered her room. As she closed the door behind her, she swallowed down the lump that was in her throat. What in the world had she and her mother gotten into here? And would she be able to get them through it with their finances, minds and hearts intact?

* * *

After a fitful night's sleep, Rebecca awoke determined to get to work, and let go of any worries or negative thoughts in regards to their future with the house. It was going to be great and she was going to build a life here with her mother in which they could be comfortable, safe and happy. The early morning sun was streaming through the dusty, old curtains in the window, promising a beautiful day, after yesterday's rain.

She heard her mother already moving around in the kitchen, so she dressed quickly and headed down to see what help she could offer.

"Good morning, Darling," her mother said as she chopped some herbs.

"Where did you get those, Mama?"

"I found a very overgrown garden, but under the overgrowth is a treasure of perennial herbs. I can get that garden cleaned up and we can use these in the food that we cook for our guests." Her mother was beaming, and Rebecca felt another jolt of hope. "So what is first on the agenda today?"

Rebecca walked over and looked at the list that they had compiled the night before. I think that we should inquire in town about a local handyman that can help us with the outside work that needs to be done, as well as some of the more complicated inside carpentry. And then, while I'm there, I can pick up the new tools we'll need, some paint and some things for the kitchen." She knew that her mother was doing her the favor of putting her in a position to be useful so that she would not worry too much about how much was to be done, and she loved her for that thoughtfulness.

"I can work on the garden and wait here for the movers to arrive with our things." Rebecca could see that he mother was antsy to get started, she so loved gardening, and having one already started was a gift from God to her for making the choice to come here. She walked over and hugged her tightly.

"Alright, Mama. After we eat I will go into town and get what we need to get started."

"Knock, knock," a women's voice carried to Rebecca and Esther through the front screen door. "Is anyone home?"

Rebecca looked at her mother, "Who could that be?" She got up and walked to the door. Standing there was round, well-groomed women in her forties, holding an enormous basket of baked goods.

"Oh, my, that looks heavy," Rebecca said, "please come in. My mother and I are just finishing breakfast in the kitchen. Would you like to join us for some tea?"

The woman was slightly out of breath as she walked through the kitchen and set down her basket on the table. "Oh thank you, I have just eaten and had plenty of coffee, but if you don't mind my sitting for a moment to catch my breath, I would appreciate that."

Esther nodded and Rebecca gestured to her own empty chair, "Please have a seat. My name is Rebecca Miller, and this is my mother, Esther."

"I'm Abigail Jones from next door. My family and I live in the farm house around the curve in the road. I heard that you would be arriving today and I wanted to welcome you. I know that the house is in disrepair, but I know that you ladies will do wonderful things with it. I heard talk of you wanting to open up a bed and breakfast here. Is that true?"

"Yes, it is," said Esther.

"That is wonderful for the neighborhood, though I hope that it brings in the right sort of people. We don't want a criminal element attracted to our little town."

Rebecca had to work hard to stifle a laugh. "Mrs. Jones..."

"Abigail, please."

"Abigail, we plan on making this a very reputable establishment with all of the required permits. Amish-run bed and breakfasts do not tend to attract much crime."

"Of course, of course." She waved her hand in the air, as if she were not the one that had brought the possibility up. "Do you know any of the Amish people here in town?"

It always amused Rebecca how outsiders thought that all Amish people in the country would know one another simply because they were Amish. There were so many different communities and locations, but to others they all looked the same. "I'm afraid not. We have just arrived here and my father's family is no longer in the area. I am sure that we will meet people as we settle into the community a bit more."

"Well, I can tell you that your closest Amish neighbor is Lucas King. He lives on the other side of me in his family's farm house." She waited for a reaction, and when she got none, she continued "now that is a sad story." Her voice was one of put-on sympathy, and Rebecca didn't want to engage her in what she was sure would be gossip, but she also didn't want to be impolite to the first person that they had met in Pennsylvania.

"How so?" Esther said, obviously sensing her daughter's hesitancy. She didn't gossip anymore than her daughter did, but she also knew the value of having good relationships with neighbors, especially ones that would gossip about them if they were not careful.

"Well, about five years ago, he was courting a young Amish girl from the community. The two of them had grown up together and seemed inseparable. Everyone said that it was going to just be a logical step on their path together for them to marry and start a family. That seems to be the way that things are done in your world." She looked at the women for confirmation, and while it was a vast oversimplification of the character of their relationships and family lives, they both nodded to allow her to continue with her story. "So they seemed to be well on their way to planning the wedding, as my friend Missy Freeburn who owns the local dress shop confirmed. Then one day some out-of-town Amish folks rolled into town from somewhere else...not sure where. They spent a few weeks here visiting...I don't really know the circumstances, as those folks are very private." She gave a sideways glance, maybe wondering if Rebecca and Esther would be the same way. "Anyhow, at the end of their stay there, didn't that girl roll off with them, planning on marrying one of the boys that she had just met in their group! It was a scandal and an embarrassment, not to mention a shock. That's not typical Amish behavior, is it?"

Rebecca and Esther stared, open-mouthed and shocked. It was certainly not typical Amish behavior, and the fact that this outsider was gossiping about like it was entertainment was an even greater surprise. Usually anything like this that happened would be kept in the community and silent. "It certainly is not typical, Abigail," Esther said gently. "May I ask how you know so many of the details of this young man's heartbreak?"

"This is a small town, and the Amish community isn't that big. When big things like that happen, everyone tends to find out about it. "Well, and not to gossip, but that poor boy just fell right off the wagon after she left."

"What do you mean?" Rebecca said, now too intrigued not to ask questions.

"He was in the pub nearly every night for a year!"

"Oh, please, don't tell us anymore," Esther groaned. Rebecca understood her mother's request. Such heartbreak and such shame were not something that they wanted to know about.

Not understanding that Esther truly wanted her to stop speaking, Abigail continued, "but that boy is fine now. It's been five years, though he is one of the least friendly people that I know. But he's turned his life around. In fact, he is the local handyman for the county. "Rebecca and Esther looked at each other with wide eyes. This was going to be a complication that they had not counted on.

"Well then, ladies, I think that I will leave you to your work. Going to be a busy few months for you, I think." She looked around with what Rebecca could only interpret as a self-satisfied smile.

"Thank you for dropping by, Abigail, and thank you for the food basket." Esther slowly guided Abigail toward the door with her own body language.

"It is my pleasure. I can't wait to see what you do with the old place." With that she passed through the front door, gave a little wave and waddled down the stairs and back to her own property.

"I guess we know who to go to for town gossip," Esther said with a chuckle.

"And who to avoid if we ever find ourselves in possession of secrets," Rebecca added with a shake of her head. People like Abigail Jones enjoyed stirring up trouble and they were good at knowing what buttons to press. She would have to be careful of that one.

"True. But that poor man she spoke of..."

"Mama, I don't know that I would believe everything that she said. Sometimes gossip is just idle stories with no basis in fact. There are always more sides to a story." Gossip was never high on her list of favorite pastimes. And people who gossiped made her very uncomfortable.

"That's true. And really it is none of our business what happened to this poor man. Though, if he is sad or angry, that is something that may affect us, because we will likely need his services."

"Mama, don't judge before we meet him. He may be a perfectly fine gentleman that Mrs. Jones just finds odd because our culture is so different from hers. The story may not even be true. Don't despair. If you wait for our things and work in the garden, I will head to town and get the list that we spoke about. I will be back this afternoon."

* * *

Rebecca's first impression of the little town was that it was a quaint, little corner of the world, full of charm and character. She smiled to herself. This would be the perfect complement to their bed and breakfast that she wanted to have a similar quaint, charming feel. She couldn't deny to herself, though she would to her mother, and anyone else that asked, that she was absolutely terrified about how they were going to pull this off. The time-line they had settled on, even if the home had been in better shape, was a lot to take on. With the amount that they needed to do, and the work that was going to go into it was going to mean that she would be sleeping very little over the next four months. The height of winter would bring lots of business if they could be ready to go. But there was a huge "if" there, and she knew it.

She entered the hardware store first and took in the shelves packed with everything from tools to dish detergent.

"Can I help you, young lady?" A kind-faced old man in a red t-shirt, covered by olive green overalls popped up from behind the counter, surprising her.

"Oh my," she said on an exhale. "You startled me."

The old man chuckled. "Sorry about that. My wife is always telling me that I'm too abrupt, whatever that means."

His eyes sparkled with humor and Rebecca immediately like him. "No harm done. My name is Rebecca Miller. My mother and I have just moved into the old Miller farmhouse and are going to be fixing it up over the next couple of months."

He rubbed his chin and nodded. "I've heard speak of it."

"I'm sure that you have. It seems like this small town has a pretty active, um, social network."

"They gossip like old hens." He stated it in such a matter-of-fact tone that she had to laugh.

"Well, that is good to know, Mr..."

"My name is Joe Stone. Call me Joe, everyone does."

"Okay, Joe. I have a big list of things that I am going to need to purchase in order to start work on the house. I have some tools available, but I will need to purchase a number of tools, large amounts of paint and a bunch of other supplies."

She handed him the list and he smiled. "Well, Ms. Miller, you have just made my day. I have most of it in stock, but may need to order some of it too."

"No problem. I will take what you have and then we can work out what you need to order. Do you think that you might be able have the items delivered out to the house today? It would be a huge help, as it would allow for me to get started right away."

"Absolutely. I will have a couple of my boys here pull the order. We could be out to the house by two o'clock. Would that work?"

"Oh, Joe, that would be perfect." She added a couple of final items to the list that she thought of at the last minute while she had been gazing around the store.

"I will take a few minutes to write you up an invoice right now," Joe said. He seemed almost giddy, likely from the prospect of the money that he would be making on her project. She could have purchased the items she needed at a larger store, but she always wanted to support the local community wherever she lived. After all, these were her neighbors, and when they succeeded, she succeeded. It was a simple lesson that her father had taught her before he died.

"Thank you, Joe." She poked around the shelves and mentally catalogued ideas for future projects, once the basics were fixed up.

"Alright, here you go. The items on top are what we have here now, and we will deliver to you today. The items in the bottom section are what we will order and get to you later this week. You can pay for all of it now or split it. It doesn't matter to me. I know that you are not going anywhere." He chuckled at his own joke and handed the handwritten list over.

"I will take care of it all now to make it easier. As she completed the paperwork, she asked Joe, "Incidentally, I was wondering if you might have the name of a local handyman that could help me and my mother with the project at the house. The majority of the work would be on the outside, with a few projects needing attention on the inside, like a staircase banister. My mother and I are going to do the cleaning, painting and simple carpentry tasks, but I will need to hire someone for the things I am not qualified to do."

Joe looked up from what he was doing and smiled. "I know of someone that might be able to help you, but you need to be able to deal with someone who might be less than friendly. Can you do that?"

She grimaced, but nodded. "I will deal with whatever I have to as long as he is skilled, meets deadlines and does an honest day's work."

"He does all of that. In fact, he's one of your lot – Amish, that is." There was no judgment in his tone as he continued. "Very skilled, been doing it for years, just not the happiest guy to be around. Doesn't bother me, but I wanted to make sure I was upfront with you."

"His name wouldn't happen to be Lucas King, would it?"

Joe looked surprised. "Luke. Yeah, do you know him?"

"No, but Abigail Jones paid us a visit today and filled us in on his history. We were very sorry to hear it."

"Gah," he threw his hands in the air in disgust. "That old biddy. If she keeps spreading stories how is that boy ever going to move on? Don't believe everything that you hear about it. Most of the stories that are circulating are not true. Like, the story about his turning to the drink. Not true. He was working for a year, fixing up the pub for my brother-in-law." He looked at her with sincere eyes. "Listen, don't judge him by what she told you. Gossip is what the serpent uses to turn folks against each other."

"Don't worry, Joe, I never believe gossip. I prefer to meet people before I make any judgments about who they are or what I think of them. Gossip is not something that I enjoy."

He nodded with respect in his eyes. "I think that we are going to get along just fine, young lady. I will have the delivery out to you by two. And will ask Luke to come out and meet with you ladies. You couldn't do better with anyone else in the county."

"Thank you, Joe." She smiled and left the store.

Her next stop was the grocery store and then she planned to browse a bit in a sweet little tourist shop, getting ideas for accent pieces that might fit into the character that she had in mind for the B&B. She swung into the small shop and smiled at the woman at the counter. The woman did not smile back, in fact, if she was not mistaken, the woman actually glared at her.

After browsing for a few minutes she looked up at the front and noticed the shop keeper staring at her. Uncomfortable, she decided that she would leave, when the woman finally spoke. "You're one of the women that moved into the Miller farm, aren't you?" Her tone made Rebecca feel as if there was acid rolling off the woman's tongue, and coming straight toward her.

"Yes. I'm Rebecca Miller. My mother, Esther and I are moving into my family's home."

She huffed a breath. "Your family's home, huh? Is that why it's been abandoned for over a year? It's an eye sore you know?"

Rebecca was taken aback, she couldn't believe what she was hearing. "Well, that's why we plan on fixing it up."

"Oh, and you just *have* to do that by creating a B&B?" The sarcasm was vicious and Rebecca flinched.

"It's a dream that my mother and I have shared for years."

"Well, we don't really want your kind here. We already have a B&B in town. My sister owns it and she's not some weirdo Amish spinster, she's a regular person. You think you're going to run her out of business, do you?" So this was going to be the level of competition in town. She couldn't believe their bad luck.

"I have no intention of doing so. We are simply planning on sharing our home with visitors. So many people pass through this county during the year, there could be a dozen B&B's in town and not one of them would hurt for business."

"Whatever. Just know that you are not welcomed by everyone here. My sister and I are going to make sure that you don't cause us any trouble." She raised her eyebrows in a silent challenge. Rebecca had never been one to back down, but she also was not one for physical altercations. However, the urge to hit this woman was strong. She shook her head, spun on her heel and left the store.

She heard a harsh "don't come back now, you hear?" as the door shut. She walked steadily until she was out of site of the store windows and then paused to take a deep breath. Things had just gone from bad to worse. She had hoped that this plan they had would not step on any local toes, and now she knew that it was a vain hope. She was going to have to stand up to locals that would think nothing of bullying a "weak" Amish woman. Little did they know that she had no intention of backing down. Like Joe had said, she wasn't going anywhere.

Rebecca was pleased to see several men working on bringing their belongings into the house. Someone had thought to put a piece of plywood over the holes in the porch so no one would misstep and get hurt, and it looked like they were actually almost done. She smiled and waved as she passed. "Is my mother out in the garden?" she asked. One of men nodded and pointed and she waved in thanks.

As she rounded the corner of the house, she was amazed to see that her mother had made significant progress in the garden. The tangle of weeds was cleared out and piled in an old wheelbarrow that she guessed her mother had found in the garden shed. There were several kinds of herbs uncovered, and even a few squash.

"Hey, Mama. The garden looks amazing."

Her mom beamed at her with dirt on both cheeks and her forehead. "Thank you, Darling. How was the trip to town?"

"Well, I got the order placed for all the supplies we need. Most will be here this afternoon and the rest will come later this week." She hesitated.

"And?" How did her mother always know when there was more?

"Well I ran into a little trouble in town. I didn't catch her name, but I went into a little touristy shop for ideas on décor, and the woman challenged me. Apparently her sister has the only B&B in town and they are not happy that we are here doing this. She didn't offer specific threats, but it comes down to the fact that they are probably going to make this process as difficult as they have the power to make it."

"Oh my, that's unfortunate." Rebecca opened her mouth to answer, but was interrupted.

"Hello?" A tall, strong-shouldered man was approaching them from the front of the house. His dark brown eyes were nearly black, and his face was so perfectly chisled that it almost seemed as if he were carved from stone. "I'm looking for Rebecca Miller. Joes sent me over about some work you want done."

"Mr. King, yes. Thank you for coming at such short notice."

"Nothing else going on today." He muttered as he eyed her offered hand, but didn't make a move to take it.

Rebecca and Esther exchanged a look of confusion, but Rebecca moved on. "Well, that's fortunate for us. I ..."

He held up his hand. "Look, not to be rude, but let's not do that small talk conversation, where we get to know each other. Tell me what is it you want done, and I will tell you how much it will cost to do it."

Rebecca was dumbstruck. She'd never had a man, much less one from her own community, be so abrupt without provocation. Idly she wondered if he might be connected to the other B&B owners somehow. But, she had a job to do, and he came highly recommended, so she began showing him the list of tasks that she needed completed, and specifying the timeline in which she wanted them done. She began on the outside of the house and then worked her way in.

They ended on the front porch. "And finally, I need this porch sturdy and safe. I don't know if it will need to be completely torn down and replaced or if you might be able to salvage what doesn't look to be rotted on the surface.

When she finished he kept writing on his pad, where he had been taking notes the whole time she spoke. He finished writing and looked up at her. "And you actually think that between me and you two doing the work that this place will be up and running in four months?"

The tone of his questions brought red to her cheeks. He made her feel like a ridiculous child with his raised eyebrows and sarcasm. "That's the hope," she said, keeping her voice even to mask the hurt.

"I will be back tomorrow to start work. I will have an estimate for the work in its entirety at that point. I don't want to be micromanaged, or nickel-and-dimed. I'll meet your deadlines if you leave me be and stay out of my way." With that he turned and walked down the steps and walked away.

"Well, that went well." My mother came out from inside the shadowed doorway of the front door. She had a small smile on her face. "Do you still want to use him?"

Rebecca stared after his retreating form. He was rude and pushy, that was true. But Joe had said that he was the best. And if she had to be honest with herself, there was something about the man that she was drawn to. Besides the fact that his figure was quite attractive and his strength would make a woman feel safe, if he were on her side, there was a beauty to his eyes, hidden behind the confrontational wall. She longed to break through whatever it was keeping him so cold. "I think so, Mama."

"Oh boy, I know that look. You get that look when you are trying to tame stray animals that come into our yard. But darling, he is not one that is going to be easily tamed. There is too much hurt there." Rebecca nodded in silent agreement. He wasn't one that would be easily touched, but she still felt drawn to see how this all played out.

* * *

The next morning brought another beautiful, sunny day, and made Rebecca eager to get started. Her mother, exhausted from all of her gardening the day before, was not awake at this pre-dawn hour, so Rebecca chose to get started working in a room at the far end of the hallway. She started cleaning and patched some holes in the wall. By the time she was done hanging painter's tape, the sun was coming up over the horizon. She opened the paint that they had selected for the room and got to work. First the ceiling, then the trim, then the walls. It was hard work, but she loved the quiet, as well as the sense of accomplishment.

As she finished up the first coat, she heard her mother shuffle down the steps and into the kitchen. Not a moment later she heard a man's voice speaking with her mother. She made her way down the hallway to listen.

"It's Esther, please. No need to be so formal."

"Okay. Well, I am going to start on the loose shingles on the roof. I want to make sure that you are set up there because it seems like rain may roll in later this afternoon." She heard the door shut behind him.

"You can come down now, Darling." Her mother laughed lightly. "He certainly is abrupt, isn't he?"

Rebecca nodded and they got to preparing breakfast. Over their meal they spoke about details for the work and decided that Esther would finish the garden before she got to helping with the inside of the house, especially if it really was going to rain. Rebecca would continue going room to room and finish what she could for the day.

The day passed quickly and Rebecca saw very little of Luke. The rain did indeed come and the storm darkened the house enough to require Rebecca to light the lamps in the house. As she lit the one in the front entrance, Luke came charging in, drenched and dripping. He ran into Rebecca, not having seen her and grabbed her waist to keep her from fall backwards from the impact.

She let out a small squeak of surprise and lifted her hands to grab his arms. The muscles were strong and she could make out the outline of muscles where the water had soaked his shirt. She knew she should let go, but couldn't bring herself to do it. And he didn't let go either. They just stood there in the dim lamp glow, staring at each other in a mesmerized state.

A knock at the door made them both jump and broke the spell. Luke backed away and busied himself drying off with a towel that Esther had hung by the front door for him. Rebecca opened the door to find a suspicious-looking man in a black suit, grinning at her. His eyes darted behind her, looking into the house.

"Can I help you?" She said as she moved forward to intentionally block his view.

"Why yes, Mrs. Esther Miller, I presume?" His voice made the hairs on the back of her neck stand on end.

"No, sorry."

"Then you must be her lovely daughter, Rebecca?"

"You can call me Ms. Miller, she said in disgust. She heard Luke actually laughing low behind the door, and she had to summon her willpower to not join him. There was something infectious about bringing out laughter in a man that was so guarded.

The man locked eyes with her, and she could tell that her comment had thrown him off. "Ms. Miller, I am Anthony Crook. " He handed her his business card. "I represent Crook Estate Sales and Antiquities, and I believe that I could be of some service to you."

"Is that so, Mr. Crook? How so?"

"We are the county's most esteemed antiquities company and we work with families who may want to liquidate some of their family's unwanted assets."

"Well, thank you for stopping by, Mr. Crook, but nothing here, in my family's home, is unwanted." She went to shut the door, but he stuck his foot in the way and said, "Perhaps I could just come inside and give you an estimate of what some of your items are worth."

Rebecca was about to open her mouth the tell him to get off her porch when the door was pulled from her hand and Luke stepped out between her and the unwanted visitor.

"I believe that the lady said that she would not be in need of your services," Luke growled at the man. "Kindly take your foot out of her doorway and leave."

Anthony Crook took a step back and nodded. There was definite fear in his eyes, but he recovered quickly when he looked back at Rebecca. "If you change your mind, you have my card."

Luke closed the door after he walked away and when it clicked he looked at Rebecca. "Was his last name really Crook?" he said flatly.

She looked at him and nodded. "Yep." They held eyes for a few seconds and then both broke out into fits of laughter. They laughed until it hurt and Rebecca thought to herself that it felt so wonderful just to laugh.

* * *

It took Luke two months to finish the work that needed to be done on the outside of the house. He had repaired the roof and broken siding boards. He had found some old shutters, repaired them, and hung them in all the windows. He had repaired the porch, and even dug out some old rocking chairs he discovered in the basement. He brought in a small crew that repainted the house with a gleaming white finish. Under the direction of Esther, a landscaping crew had repaired the front walk and cleaned up the overgrown parts of the property surrounding the house. Her mother had tackled the gardens and fountain, and through all these efforts, Rebecca actually saw the makings of a gorgeous house with some pretty amazing curb appeal. While all of that had been happening outside, she had been busy inside, going room to room – cleaning, painting and repairing. Once and a while she would need to call Luke in to help her. She didn't like to do so because it would take away from his outside work. But when he did come in, he was quiet and professional, not rude like he had been when they first met. He wasn't, however, friendly and talkative. And the worst part was that when he was working, she couldn't keep her eyes off of him. His form and skills fascinated her. She found him absolutely beautiful.

The project was on schedule and everyone was tired, but focused. Rebecca had three more visits from Anthony Crook. "Call me," he would always say when she would politely decline his request to come into the home to look around.

As they entered into the third month of work, Luke's duties were now primarily inside the home, so Rebecca and he ran into each other more often. The fell into a rythym where she brought him tea first thing in the morning, and he made coffee to keep them going in the afternoon. He would laugh each time Anthony Crook left. "Doesn't he get it that we don't have phones here?" This fun side to Luke only intrigued Rebecca more.

One evening Esther invited Luke to stay for dinner. "You got the stove working properly and finally fixed the cellar door. Let me make you a home-cooked meal." He had finally relented, realizing that she was not going to take "no" for an answer.

"Luke, thank you for all of the fine work that you have been doing," Esther said as they sat at the table. "It really is outstanding in its quality."

Luke grunted, very obviously uncomfortable.

A knock at the front door saved him from having to comment any further. Rebecca answered the door and was shocked to see the shop-keeper that had threatened her when she had first moved to town. "We aren't open for business," she said before she could think better of it.

"Funny," the woman said sarcastically.

"What do you want?" She didn't want the woman spoiling her dinner with Luke and her mother.

"Who is it?" Luke asked as he rounded the corner and stopped dead in his tracks. "Lillian." Rebecca recognized his guarded tones as what he had used on her and Esther when he first came to them for work. His walls were back up. "What are you doing here?"

"I heard you were working here and I wanted to see for myself. How could you? How could you help people that will hurt us?"

His eyes flashed and he stepped forward, leaning toward her. "There is no us," he growled. "You gave 'us' up when you made your choice to leave the community for that man. What, did he leave you?" He sneered with distain as he spoke.

"Luke, please now." She purred. "I left the community, but I couldn't bear to be away from you."

"Lillian, that just isn't true. You came back to live with your sister with your tail between your legs. You know that if she hadn't left our community, she wouldn't have been able to take you in. You put her in an impossible position."

It was her turn to be angry. "What do you care for my sister? I didn't see you standing up for her when she needed you."

"You need to leave." He said, cutting off any further comment. "We're done here. The Millers have every right to open this establishment, and in fact, your sister is excited about the healthy competition.

"That's not true. Why do you say that?" Her eyes shifted side to side as she crossed her arms in front of her.

"I spoke with her the other day. I check in on her every few weeks, which is something you don't know. You would know that if you cared for her in any way other than a provider of shelter while you consider your next move."

"Dears," Esther came up between them, "this is not the place for this discussion. Lillian, is it? You need to go home and find a more appropriate place and time to speak with Lucas. Have a good night."

She gently shut the door as Lillian stood with her mouth hanging open. "I'm done eating and am a little tired. I am going to head up to bed. Why don't you two kids wait for her to leave and then take some tea out onto the porch? It is a lovely night to gaze at the stars."

Rebecca fixed tea, and when they were sure that the coast was clear, they headed out to sit.

"'So?" She started.

"So." He was silent for a moment and then launched into the story. "Lillian and I grew up together here in our community. The next natural step was marriage and a family. I know that she wanted more, but I didn't let myself understand what that would really mean. People in town have some romanticized idea that she rode off in the back of a wagon with another community, but really what happened was that she met a man outside of our faith, fell in love with him, turned her back on all of us, and ran away. I was devastated and my faith was shaken. Not even a year later she was back. He had deserted her, who knows why, and she needed someone to help her. Instead of coming back and pleading for help from the community, or me, she convinced her sister to turn her back on all of us, as well. So they stayed nearby and opened a B&B. But they no longer are a part of us. She is angry that I do not want to leave the community and come with her, but I have no intention of turning my back on our faith. So really, that is why she was here. She is upset that I am helping you. She is jealous that someone like you is living the life of choices that she wanted while still being a part of our community. You are an amazing woman, and she knows that I have respect for everything that you are doing here, and how you are. And that hurts her."

Rebecca nodded, speechless. She held out her hand and he took it. They sat and silently watched the stars until it was time for him to head home. As she watched him walk away, she knew that there would be no turning back. She was his now.

* * *

Rebecca, Esther and Luke worked hard and were able to meet the goal date of four months for the complete restoration. Over dinner on their last night of work, Rebecca proudly announced that they were fully booked for their first weekend. They celebrated with good food and light-hearted tales about the funny things that occurred during the repairs.

"Ladies, I also wanted to tell you something important. Lillian has decided to move on. She contacted some distant family in another community and they are willing to take her in if she returns to the faith and works with them. She will not be a problem anymore."

"What about her sister?" Esther asked with concern.

Luke smiled and his eyes lit up. "She is happier than I have ever seen her. She loves her life and her business. She misses certain parts of the community, but she has met a kind man from town and they are courting."

Everyone smiled at that and then the table grew silent.

"I just wanted to tell you how in awe I am of you two getting all of this done. I never thought that I would see this done on time, with complete occupancy. You Millers are a force of nature."

Esther smiled and took his hand. "You are sweet, but we could not have done this without you. And on that note, my old bones are tired and I am going to head to bed. It's another good night for star gazing," she said with a wink at Rebecca behind Luke's back.

Rebecca and Luke headed out to the porch to enjoy the gorgeous crisp night air. They brought blankets to ward off the cold that nipped at their extremities. As they sat in silence, Rebecca felt herself drawn toward Luke, as she had been for so long.

"Rebecca, can I ask you something?" His voice was uncharacteristically cautious.

"Anything."

"If I were to reach over and take your hand would that be okay?"

She didn't answer, but reached over and took his hand.

"And if I were to kiss your lips lightly, would you object?"

Again, she didn't answer, but leaned toward him and let him move in for a gentle kiss.

"And if I were to give you this, what would you say?"

She looked over at him and saw that he was holding a beautiful ring.

Tears sprang to her eyes and she reached out her left hand in silent response.

He slipped the ring on and the watched the stars until they couldn't stand the cold any longer.

"This is just the beginning, Rebecca. I love you, and we will have so many more nights to hold hands and gaze at the stars.

She smiled and leaned against his strong arm, feeling the familiar physical pull toward him.

She was his and now he was hers – a match fated in the stars at the Peaceful Farm Bed and Breakfast.

RACHEL

The air on her face was biting at her cheeks but she barely noticed it. A feeling of contentment had washed over her and the beauty of the picturesque landscape filled her with a joy she had never known.

Someone was calling her name and she whirled around, her skirt swirling around her ankles, a small smile on her face.

"Rachel!" he called again and she turned in the opposite direction, scanning the field at her back. Her dark hair was longer than it had ever been, cast in two long braids along either shoulder, a dramatic contrast to the white of her apron.

Despite the snow on the ground, her feet were bare and suddenly, she was painfully aware of how cold she had grown.

Gone was the sense of comfort in which she had been enveloped as something sinister filled the air instead.

"Rachel!" his voice was further away than it had been and again she spun but she no longer felt a sense of peace but an unsettling panic.

"Rachel!" the cry was desperate now, demanding and she twirled, a full circle, trying to identify the source.

Someone shoved her from behind and she gasped.

"Rachel!" The voice was directly in her ear now.

Her cobalt blue eyes flew open and she stared up at the furious face of the resident hovering above her.

"Are you kidding me?" Dr. Levin snapped. "You're taking a nap? Get up!"

Her heart racing, Rachel swung her legs over the side of the cot in the on-call room and rubbed her eyes, trying to shake off the dream.

"What happened?" she asked, jumping to her feet. She peered at her pager, her brow furrowing. It was unlike her to sleep through the vibration of the device but as she glanced at the screen, she saw that no one had paged her.

What is he doing in here? No one is looking for me.

"Car accident on Highway 80. Three badly injured. One dead."

Rachel hurried to follow the surly doctor from the room, trying to focus.

"Why wasn't I paged?" she asked and he cast her an annoyed look.

"I am telling you, aren't I? Why do you need to be paged?" he growled. "Why do you need to make everything difficult and ask stupid questions?"

Rachel had been a nurse at Saint Francis Memorial in San Francisco for two years. In that time, she had grown friendly with most of the ER staff. It was not hard to do with her sunny personality and warm smile but Dr. Levin was an anomaly.

He seemed to hate Rachel from the first minute he had laid eyes on her, going out of his way to make her life miserable.

His attitude was commonplace and both doctors and nurses rued having to work their shifts with him.

"Can you walk a little faster, please? People's lives are at stake while you take in the scenery," the resident yelled back, from five paces ahead.

Rachel bit the insides of her cheeks and rushed after him, pushing their way into the bustling emergency room.

It was her third double shift that week and she was exhausted. The nap she had been taking was the first sleep she had in over twenty hours and it had only lasted twenty minutes and been plagued by the strange dream.

As they arrived at the ambulance bay, she realized that the busses hadn't arrived yet.

"They aren't here yet?" she asked aloud.

"Oh, sorry," Dr. Levin snapped sarcastically. "Did you want to go back and take a nap until they get here?"

The other staff waiting gave him a reproving look, his sour attitude notorious among the others but Dr. Levin seemed impervious to their silent scolding.

Nancy, the head night nurse gave Rachel a warm smile as if to say, "don't worry about it" but Rachel had long since learned to deal with Dr. Levin's nastiness.

She smiled back at Nancy with false bravado.

It was nobody's business that Dr. Levin made her feel small and inept.

In minutes, the ambulances roared into port and the physicians were ready.

Rachel kept her ears perked for instructions, stepping out of the way to allow the doctors to do their jobs.

"Are you just going to stand there? Get this boy 5 milligrams of morphine stat!" Dr. Levin barked at her and humiliation colored Rachel's face. He was the only doctor who questioned her work ethic.

Swallowing her anger, Rachel turned to oblige his request, returning a moment later with a vial. She hurried toward the broken patient who was writhing in pain, moaning as tears slid down his cheeks. His shin bone was protruding from his leg and there was a deep gash on his chest.

"Oh, it hurts so bad," he cried. "Please, please help me!"

"Shh," Rachel murmured, preparing his vein. "You're going to feel better in a minute but you have to be still."

She steadied his arm to inject the needle when something caught her eye.

Quickly, she put the needle on the instrument tray and picked up his wrist.

"Please!" he moaned. "Make it stop!"

"Nurse King, are you going to administer that today?" Dr. Levin yelled, his face turning red with anger.

"I just – "Rachel protested, holding up the boy's slender wrist.

"Just give me that and get out of here."

Before Rachel could finish her statement, the boy fainted from the pain.

"Great! Nice work, Rachel. You're the most incompetent nurse I have ever seen," Dr. Levin raged, plunging the needle into the patient's arm.

"No!" Rachel gasped. "No! You're going to kill him!"

Dr. Levin turned away from her, ignoring her words and back to dealing with the bleeding gash on his chest.

"Dr. Levin!" she screamed.

"Nurse King, get out of here," he growled but Rachel didn't budge.

"No! He's going to go into anaphylactic shock! He's allergic to opiates."

She pointed at the medical alert bracelet on the patient's arm.

Dr. Levin went pale, shaking his head in disbelief and Rachel felt herself grow lightheaded.

Suddenly, his head whipped up and his eyes narrowed into slits.

"What did you do?" he hissed. Shocked, Rachel couldn't answer.

"You're incompetent! You'll never work in another hospital again!"

"Me?" she echoed, choking. "You're the one who – "

"Get out of here before you do more damage!" he roared, attracting the attention of all the other staff. "This is unforgiveable!"

Rachel backed away uncomprehendingly.

But I didn't do anything! I tried to stop him!

It was at that moment she realized that she was about to be blamed for what had happened.

"This is crap, Rachel! You need to fight this!"

Rachel stifled a sigh. It was the same conversation they had at least twenty times in the past three weeks.

"There's nothing left to fight, Cara. I've been stripped of my nursing licence. I can't practice in the state of California anymore."

"No! Dr. Levin is the devil! You can't let him get away with this!" her roommate insisted. "How can he do this?"

The question was also not foreign to Rachel; it had plagued her day and night since being called up on her review.

"They didn't believe me, pure and simple. Whose word were the going to take? A new nurse or a resident who had been at Memorial for seven years?"

"He's been written up like a million times!" Cara protested. "How can they disregard his history – oh Rach, I am so sorry I keep bringing this up but it is so unfair!"

Rachel finally turned to face her, smiling kindly.

"It's okay, Cara," she promised. "Maybe this is the universe's way of telling me I wasn't cut out for nursing after all. Two years in and I already feel like I'm burning out."

Yet as she said the words, there was a deep knife stabbing into her heart.

Rachel thought of how many hours she had worked studying, working two jobs to put herself through college.

And after college, working eighty or sometimes ninety-hour weeks.

The quest to get where she wanted to be had been excruciating and Dr. Levin had snatched it away with one swipe to save his own skin.

It was over before it had even really begun.

The only saving grace was that the young man had not suffered any long-term damage because of Dr. Levin's mistake.

If I hadn't brought it to his attention, he would have killed the boy.

Rachel knew it was only a matter of time before the doctor did kill someone.

"You can't go back to New York," Cara said dejectedly as Rachel continued to pack her bags. Rachel smiled tightly.

"I can't really afford to stay here without a job," she reminded her friend.

"You'll get another job, Rach. Just hang in there and start looking. You made up your mind without thinking it through entirely. I can cover the rent for – "

"No." There was a finality in Rachel's tone.

What had happened at the hospital had left her badly scarred and she knew she needed to distance herself from San Francisco for a while.

"No, Cara. Thank you for the offer but I think it's best that I go home to my mom and dad for a while. Clear my mind, you know?"

Cara nodded slowly but Rachel could see she did not understand.

Rachel didn't blame her for her confusion; she wasn't sure she comprehended her own willingness to leave either.

I'm burnt out. I need to regroup, collect my thoughts and figure things out. Maybe I'll end up back here but for now, I have to go.

"Walk me to the car?" she asked Cara with feigned cheer and her roommate sighed, nodding.

"Do I have a choice?" she replied sadly.

"Not if you want a really good hug."

Rachel picked up her oversized duffle bag and Cara reached for the last two boxes in the otherwise empty room.

The made their way to the U-Haul and loaded it.

"Will you call me when you get where you're supposed to be?" Cara asked, pulling Rachel into a tight embrace.

Rachel swallowed and nodded but she could not answer.

She wondered if she would ever find the place she was supposed to be.

She stretched out her long legs against the floral print of the comforter.

"No, mom, I'm fine, I swear," she said into the receiver. "I'll be home around noon tomorrow."

Rachel listened as her mother rattled off a list of precautions and rolled her eyes, a mixture of affection and annoyance tickling her stomach.

"Yes, I will make sure to eat...no, don't worry about the snow. I checked the weather before I left California...yes, the truck is reliable...okay mom, I love you too. See you then."

She replaced the earpiece on its cradle and sighed, flopping back against the pillows.

She had been driving for two straight days, stopping only for sleep and while she had initially thought it would be a depressing trip, Rachel found herself enjoying the time to herself.

How long has it been since I've been embraced by silence? She wondered. She had a hard time recalling the last time.

A fleeting thought of childhood slipped through her mind but she missed it before she could catch it.

She had the dream again, where she was standing in the field, in the snow with someone calling her name.

It was one she had experienced many times over the years but Rachel had never been able to make sense of it.

Forget about the dream, she told herself. *Forget about everything. Turn off your brain and watch television. How long has it been since you've been able to do that without feeling guilt?*

The idea was appealing and she reached for the remote control, flipping idly through the channels. She settled on a light-hearted sitcom but she was asleep before it ended twenty minutes later as if she inherently sensed that the next day would require all her strength.

That night, she did not dream.

"Hey ya! Hey ya!" she scream-sang at the top of her lungs, coasting down Interstate 80. The radio blasted the song but it could not drown out the terrible singing coming from Rachel's vocal chords.

The window was down, despite the freeze in the February day but to Rachel, it was exhilarating.

Wow! She thought. *How long has it been since I've done this? I feel so free, so...unencumbered by everything right now.*

A pessimistic side of her asked how long the euphoria would last.

She decided not to question it, turning up the radio to block out her own dark thoughts.

It was then she heard the thud.

Her heart stopped and instinctively, she slowed the car, looking in the sideview mirrors.

Oh God! Did I just hit something?

She saw nothing, turning off the stereo and steering the vehicle to the side of the road. No sooner did the wheels touch the shoulder did another loud clunk ensue and the car lost power.

Her heart pounding, Rachel leapt from the driver's seat and ran up the shoulder to ensure she had not run anything over.

Relieved that nothing seemed harmed by the U-Haul, she hurried back, rubbing her hands together as the chill crept into her collar.

Well there's my answer, she thought wryly. *It was a short-lived sense of happiness but it was there.*

She crawled back into the driver's side and tried to turn over the engine but it only sputtered, coughing in protest as she attempted.

Great. Now what?

She realized she was in the middle of nowhere, rural Ohio and she silently prayed that she would get reception on her phone.

To her relief, she had weak service and she dialed the operator for help.

Not even going to try for data up here, she thought. To her chagrin, the phone would not dial out.

"Oh come on!" she groaned, jumping from the cab again. She wandered up and down the side of the road, trying over and over as she moved but she got no luck.

Soon enough, however, she saw a car driving toward her and she flagged it down.

The grey sedan slowed and the driver rolled down the window. Rachel ran toward him gratefully.

"Thanks for stopping," she breathed but as she approached, she realized that there was an Amish man in the passenger seat and a lumberjack looking fellow at the wheel.

"You all right, lady?" the driver asked, shooting his companion a strange look.

"My truck just died on me," she said. "I'm heading to New York State and I don't know this area at all. My phone has no reception."

"Yeah, this part of the interstate can be moody with the cell towers," the driver replied. "We can take you to Olena if you want. There's a garage there. Frank can help you out."

Uncertainly, Rachel eyed the unlikely pair.

"Maybe I'll just wait out here," she said, gnawing on her lower lip. "Could you let them know I'm out here?"

The man at the wheel grunted in exasperation.

"Lady, if you ain't got heat, you're gonna freeze. Just get in the car."

Perhaps Rachel had been living in the city too long but she was instantly put off by the man's tone.

"Never mind," she replied flatly. "Sorry to have bothered you."

"Miss, we are going to Olena anyway," the Amish man said quietly and for some reason, Rachel was instantly placated by the sound of his voice. "I would not feel right leaving you here alone. It is dangerous for a woman by herself."

Rachel stared at him, noting his kind green eyes and stoic nature.

She glanced back at her truck, wondering if her belongings would be safe.

You really are becoming jaded, she chided herself. *There are no highwaymen running amok in Amish country.*

"Okay, yes," she decided quickly, sensing the driver's annoyance. "I just have to grab my purse."

She hurried back to the truck and locked up, securing her keys in the depth of her purse before climbing into the back of the car with the strangers.

This is what Dateline episodes are made of, she thought, perching nervously at the edge of the seat as she stared out the window.

"What's your name?" the driver asked.

"Rachel."

"I'm Dave. This here is Samuel. We're from Millersburg."

"Nice to meet you both," Rachel told them, studying their faces. Dave was rough around the edges without a doubt, a burly man who screamed blue collar.

He just comes across as surly but I bet he's a big pussycat, she thought, turning her attention to his quiet companion.

I wonder what they are doing together?

"Where are you coming from?"

"San Francisco."

Dave let out a low whistle.

"That's a long drive for one person. What happened? Got sick of the city life?"

If only, she thought ruefully.

"Something like that." She realized how short her answers had sounded and she instantly felt ashamed.

"I'm originally from New York. My parents are still there," she added, trying to sound friendly. She could not help that her guard was still up.

Dave looked at her through the rear-view mirror and nodded.

"It's a strange route you're taking to get back to New York," he commented and Rachel cocked her head to the side.

"Is it? I swear this is the route my GPS gave. It's the first time I've driven it."

Dave gave Samuel another look which Rachel could not decipher and she felt a strange chill flow through her.

What am I missing here?

She sat back, peering into the snowy landscape and her breath caught suddenly.

It was as if she was back in her dream, staring at the same fields, spinning in circles looking for the person calling out to her.

"We're just getting into Olena," Dave called to her after a few moments. "Bentz's Auto is not far. I hope he can tow your truck. He may need help with that."

Rachel had not thought about that but she was thankful when they pulled up to the garage. Rachel climbed out of the car and paused at the passenger window which Samuel rolled down.

"Can I offer you some gas money?" she asked and Dave snorted.

"Ask Samuel," he replied chuckling and Rachel was confused but she did.

"Samuel? Can I give you some money for your troubles?"

"No," he said softly. "I wish you the best of luck with your journey."

She stared into his vivid eyes and felt as if his words meant more than she could hear.

Rachel nodded, stepping back from the car.

"Thank you. I can't tell you how much I appreciate you stopping for me."

"Be well, little lady!" Dave hollered, pulling away from the garage and Rachel watched them drive away, a strange longing in her chest.

What a strange encounter, she thought, turning back to the small white structure at her back.

She could not shake the feeling that it had meant something.

Rachel grimaced slightly, pacing around the front of the garage.

"No, mom, it's fine," she grumbled. "I don't need dad to drive here and meet me. It's just not going to be towed until tomorrow and...I told you, I'm in Olena, Ohio."

She rolled her eyes heavenward in silent plea.

"I will let you know what the mechanic says but everything is fine. I'm safe and...yes, mom, I promise – "

Her blue eyes darted upward as a familiar car pulled into the small front lot.

"I have to go, mom. Love you."

She hung up the call and stared curiously as Dave pulled the car along side of her.

Samuel rolled down the passenger side window.

"Hello," she said, curiosity lacing her words. "What are you doing here?"

"We wanted to ensure that you were all right," the Amish man said and Rachel found herself inordinately pleased.

"I won't know until tomorrow," she replied. "Dave was right; Frank the mechanic says he can't tow something that size and he can't get a flatbed until the morning."

"What will you do?" Dave called. Rachel had been asking herself the same question. She simply did not have the money to spend another night or two in a hotel but what other choice did she have?

"I – I guess I'm staying at a hotel," she sighed. "Any recommendations?"

There was a short silence and the men looked at one another.

Samuel cleared his throat.

"I have a farmhouse with many rooms," he told her quietly. "You are welcome to stay there free of charge."

Rachel blinked, stunned by the offer.

Is this generosity or something else? She wondered and guilt immediately flooded her. *Really, Rachel, you have spent far too much time in the city.*

As if reading her thoughts, Samuel continued quickly.

"I live there with my two sisters."

Rachel offered him a quick smile.

"That is very kind but are you sure I won't upset the community?"

The question was sincere but Dave howled.

"That depends; are you going to host any wild parties tonight, lady?" Dave chuckled and Rachel looked mortified. "Run moonshine? Host a poker game?"

"No of course not!" she replied indignantly but she saw that Samuel had an amused grin on his face.

"Come on, Rachel. I'm supposed to be picking someone else up in an hour."

Rachel nodded slowly, once more climbing into the back of the car, slightly overwhelmed by the strangers who had appeared seemingly from nowhere.

This time as they pulled away, Rachel instigated the conversation with the men, determined to express her appreciation.

"I think I have lived in the big city for too long," she confessed. "I had forgotten how kind folks can be in small towns."

"You get your good and bad everywhere you go," Dave replied. "Isn't that right, Samuel?"

"Yes," he agreed. "People live by their own moral code. We are all born with a sense of right and wrong. Whether we choose to adhere to it is on us."

Instantly, Dr. Levin's face popped into Rachel's mind and she was filled with bitterness.

No. He stays in San Fran where you left him. Don't let that affect this moment in your life, she warned herself. She returned her focus to her new companions.

"I imagine that you don't have much of a problem in your community," Rachel piped up. Dave laughed again and Rachel felt her cheeks turn pink.

"I'm sorry if I sound ignorant," she said quickly. "I don't know very much about Amish culture."

"I am happy to answer any questions. I am very proud of our heritage," Samuel replied easily and Rachel was grateful for his indulgence. "It is not ignorance if you are willing to learn. And to answer your question, yes, we have those who stray in our community also. God does send temptation forth to test us."

Rachel was once more filled with the sense that his words had an underlying meaning.

Am I a test for him from God?

"Your knowledge comes from living among the Amish, Dave?" Rachel asked. She cringed at her inquiries. They sounded so strange to her own ears.

"I drive for the district. The Amish do not drive themselves so I am essentially a taxi service."

Rachel paled slightly as she remembered Dave's words earlier when she had offered them money.

Why on earth would Dave stop for me on Samuel's dime? That's rude.

"I hope you're not charging him extra because you chose to stop for me," Rachel chuckled, only half-joking as she eyed Samuel.

Dave laughed his boisterous laugh again.

"I should charge him double!" Dave chortled. "I didn't want to stop at all. He insisted that we not only stop but go back and make sure you were okay. I told him you're a city girl. You'll be fine but he was worried about you."

Rachel stared at Samuel, her mouth slightly agape but he turned to look out the window, purposely avoiding her gaze.

Feeling slightly dazed, Rachel sat back.

Did God send me a guardian angel in the form of Samuel? She wondered. It certainly seemed that way.

They arrived at Samuel's farm slightly after five o'clock and Samuel nodded to Dave.

"*Danke.* Will you stop by tomorrow for Rachel?"

"I'll come around noon but I'll give Frank a ring at the shop before I head over this way. No sense in dragging her back to town if the car isn't going to be ready," Dave replied. "I'll only end up bringing her back and I'm sure she's already seen enough of me for a lifetime."

He grinned to show he was kidding.

"Would you call for me?" Rachel asked, still amazed at the good will of the men. Dave gave her a puzzled look.

"Of course, lady. We watch out for each other in these parts."

He smiled then and Rachel was sure she had never seen a lovelier smile in her life. It instantly lifted her spirits and she returned it easily.

"Thank you, Dave," she whispered, raising a hand as he nodded and drove away from the front of the house.

Alone, Rachel looked shyly at Samuel.

"This is all yours?" she asked, gesturing around the vast property. The house itself was elegant but simple and well maintained.

"Mine and my sisters, yes," he replied, extending an arm in gesture for her to approach. "Our parents left it to us when they died."

Rachel felt a stab of sadness.

"I'm sorry," she breathed as they climbed the steps to the front door. "I didn't mean to – "

Abruptly the front door flew open, startling Rachel and two young women stood beyond the screen, staring open mouthed at her.

They were both younger than Samuel, closer to Rachel's age.

"Ah, you are home," Samuel said, pulling on the exterior door. "I hope you made enough supper for a fourth. This is Rachel..."

He peered at her and Rachel cleared her nervousness from her throat, smiling quickly.

"Rachel King," she said, extending her hand toward the awe-struck girls. The took her hand, trying not to stare at her but Rachel could read the excitement in their faces.

I guess Samuel doesn't bring strange outsiders home every day, she thought wryly.

"These are my sisters, Ruth and Miriam Roth."

"Nice to meet you both," Rachel said, stepping inside the house but she had to squeeze past them.

"Welcome Rachel," Miriam said, finally recovering from her shock. "Yes, of course there is always enough food for visitors."

"Rachel will be spending the night. Please ensure there are fresh linens on the bed in the downstairs room," Samuel told them as he pulled off his boots.

Again, the sisters seemed dumbfounded but the nodded, trying to hide their emotions, ducking out of the foyer.

"Samuel, if this is a problem, I can certainly make other arrangements for the night," Rachel told him quickly. Samuel chuckled lightly and removed his hat, running his hand through his dark blonde hair.

"I assure you, it is not a problem. We have a toilet near the kitchen if you should need to wash." He pointed her in the direction and Rachel accepted the cue to go.

She entered the room where a candle was flickering, casting soft shadows along the dark wood trim and Rachel was sure she had never felt more at ease in a bathroom.

It feels like home, she thought and her brow furrowed at the idea.

How could a remote farmhouse in Amish country possibly feel like home?

She splashed cold water on her face and stared at her meteoric reflection in the mirror, she had a spark of de ja vu.

What is it about today? She asked herself. *It's like there's something in the air, something...spiritual or otherworldly.*

There was a tentative knock on the door.

"Rachel? Dinner is on the table."

She was not sure which sister it was but Rachel thanked her and dried her face and hands quickly, moving to join the Roth family.

"Please, sit," Samuel said, smiling. She slipped into a chair beside Miriam as Ruth brought the rest of the meal to the table.

"We pray before we eat, Rachel," Samuel explained. "You are not required to do so if you do not wish."

Rachel stared at them, wide eyed.

How long has it been since I've prayed? She wondered.

"I would like to join you," she told them sincerely. The sisters exchanged a small smile and lowered their heads as Samuel led grace.

As he spoke, Rachel found herself staring up at him, following the words from his lips. A true calm washed through her body.

The siblings raised their heads and began to pass around the platters of food, starting with Rachel's.

"Where are you from, Rachel?" Ruth asked politely.

"I was born in New York State but I have been living in San Francisco," she explained. "I am just on my way home to my family. My truck broke down and your brother was kind enough to offer his assistance."

A look of genuine understanding flowed through both girls as the mystery of her arrival was solved.

"Ah, what a shame," Miriam said. "Does the mechanic know what is the problem?"

"Unfortunately he can't even look at it until tomorrow."

The women made a commiserating noise in unison and Rachel was beginning to wonder if they were twins.

She looked up and met Samuel's eyes. They were bright with amusement.

"King, you say? Rachel King?" Ruth piped up suddenly and Rachel nodded. She cocked her head to the side and studied Rachel's face closely.

"Do you have any Amish roots?"

Rachel almost choked on her potatoes.

She sputtered and shook her head, reaching for some water.

"Pardon me!" she said as she caught her breath. "That went down wrong."

Samuel laughed aloud.

"I think that is Rachel's way of saying she has no ties to the Amish community, Ruthie."

But Ruth did not smile. She continued to stare at Rachel.

"No, Samuel, she's the very image of – "

"Ruth, that's enough!"

Samuel's tone startled everyone at the table equally and an uncomfortable silence ensued. Miriam jumped in to fill the void.

"What do you do, Rachel? Are you a student?"

"I am a nurse," she replied automatically. The table dropped their forks simultaneously, their mouths agape.

I should have said I was a nurse but no need to bore them with the details of my pathetic life right now.

A slow appreciation filled Samuel's eyes.

"You are a healer," he said softly. "That is very fitting."

A warm glow filled Rachel's heart and she lowered her head in embarrassment.

It seemed that every word he spoke to her made her feel light headed.

This is crazy! You can't become smitten with an Amish man you've known for an hour.

But reason didn't seem to help.

Samuel Roth had a strange hold over her, something inexplicable and Rachel was basking in the sweetness of the feeling.

Ruth set her up in the back bedroom on the main floor. It had its own fireplace and the logs crackled as they entered.

"If you should need anything, my bedroom is at the very top of the stairs."

"I have everything I need," Rachel assured her. "You have been more than kind sharing your home and food with a perfect stranger."

"I don't think you are a stranger, Rachel," Ruth muttered as she turned away.

"What do you mean?" Rachel called out to her, a peculiar feeling touching her gut. Ruth paused in the doorway.

"I think you have Amish in your blood."

She was gone before Rachel could question her further, leaving the former nurse to ponder her cryptic words.

Is that why I feel so comfortable here? Do I have Amish ancestors?

It seemed so farfetched and yet...

Weak sunlight spilled into the back room and Rachel woke, surprisingly energetic.

She had slept better than she had in longer than she could recall and she slipped from the bed, determined to make breakfast for the family before they too rose.

It's the least I can do, she thought but as she hurried into the kitchen, she saw she was already too late.

Samuel was at the sink when she entered, his long hair slightly matted from sleep.

"Oh," she said with some disappointment. "I was hoping to be up before you this morning."

He turned, his eyes twinkling.

"That would be very difficult to do," he told her. "I am a farmer after all."

Rachel chuckled.

"Let me help you," she said, stepping toward the sink but he shook his head.

"You are a guest here," he replied. "Please sit. You can keep me company if you wish. Do you drink coffee?"

"I did mention that I was a nurse, right?"

He nodded, his smile widening and Rachel was drawn in by his brilliant white smile.

"Did you ever ask yourself how you came to be here?" Samuel asked suddenly and Rachel's brow furrowed slightly.

Is this an existential question? Probably not.

"Um...well I think U-Haul had a hand in it," she murmured jokingly. Samuel approached her, placing a steaming cup of hot coffee before her.

"You chose and obscure route returning to New York," he told her softly. "Dave and I discussed it at length. There were much better ways for you to have travelled."

Rachel shrugged, unsure of what he was getting at exactly.

"The GPS is not infallible," she replied. "And I have little sense of natural direction."

Samuel began to laugh.

"I think the opposite is true," he replied softly. Rachel sat back and stared at him.

"What is going on?" she demanded. "What are you saying?"

Samuel sat at the kitchen table and stared at her, his green eyes searching her face.

"Do you remember your childhood at all?"

"Of course."

"How old is the youngest you remember?"

Rachel thought.

"Maybe five? Six?"

He nodded.

"Do you ever dream of this place?"

Goosebumps prickled her skin.

"Samuel, you're beginning to scare me," she told him honestly. "What are you talking about?"

"Rachel, you and your family were born here in Holmes County. When you were four, your parents abruptly decided to leave the community and they took you and your little sister with them. No one knows why it happened. There was speculation that your mother was shunned and your father could not live without her."

Rachel stared at him, her jaw almost at the table.

She shook her head.

"No," she protested. "There's no way. My parents haven't even taken us to church."

"Is your sister named Mary? Two years younger than you?"

Rachel felt hot and cold at the same time and she stared at him in disbelief.

It couldn't be and yet...

"How did you know?" she gasped. "How can you remember that?"

Samuel rose and offered his hand to her.

"Come," he said gently. "I want to show you something."

Reluctantly, she followed him to the front door.

They stepped onto the snowy veranda in bare feet and suddenly, Rachel saw it.

It was the field from her dream.

"That was your family's farm," Samuel told her. "You can't see it from here, but the house is slightly over the hill. Our families were neighbors for generations."

The information was overwhelming and Rachel was suddenly weak in the knees. She reached out to grasp a railing but Samuel caught her.

"I have to get out of here," she whispered, her eyes dark with fear. "If we are shunned..."

Samuel shook his head.

"You are not shunned. You have not been baptized. I am certain if you wanted to return, the Bishop could see to it that you are properly prepared for life here."

She stared at him, uncomprehendingly.

"Return?" she echoed. "What makes you think that I want to return here? I don't know anything about your culture."

"It is your culture," he reminded her. "And you make me think you want to return here. You have come here. Something has driven you back here after all these years. Your car has failed you just in the proper place. Something is speaking to you if only you'd listen."

And suddenly every word he spoke made perfect sense.

Everything which has happened has been leading up to this moment; losing my job, leaving California, driving this obscure route.

She looked at him and realized that everything she had ever wanted was in one place and it always had been; she just hadn't known where to look for it.